Good-bye to Earth

LEO P. KELLEY

A Pacemaker® Book

Fearon Education
a division of
David S. Lake Publishers
Belmont, California

A-1

SEP 8 7

THE GALAXY 5 SERIES
  Good-bye to Earth
  On the Red World
  Vacation in Space
  Dead Moon
  Where No Sun Shines
  King of the Stars

Series Director: Robert G. Bander
Designer: Richard Kharibian
Cover and illustrations: Rick Guidice

ISBN–0–8224–3201–3
Library of Congress Catalog Card Number: 78–68226
Printed in the United States of America.

1. 9 8 7 6 5

CONTENTS

CHAPTER **1**

A VERY SPECIAL DAY

She woke up and for a minute she didn't know where she was. Then she remembered. She was in her room at Space School. She had lived at Space School for the past three years.

Ellen Drake thought about those years. They had been good ones, full of hard work and many long hours of study.

She lay there in her bed thinking of what the new day that was coming would bring to her. It was still night now. She looked at the clock near the bed. Soon it would be time. Soon the sun would begin to climb into the sky. But not for more than an hour yet.

Ellen got out of bed. She ran her fingers through her short, curly blonde hair. The floor under her feet felt cold. She walked over to the window and looked up at the sky. There was no moon. But the stars were up there—white dots of light in the dark.

Looking at the stars, Ellen felt just a little bit afraid. Not of the stars. She thought of the stars as friends. But she was afraid that she might never be able to reach them. She wouldn't if she didn't pass the last test she had to take when the new day came.

She turned away from the window and crossed the room. She went to the mirror and looked at her smooth face and large blue eyes. She couldn't seem to stand still. She thought about getting back into bed. But she knew that if she did she wouldn't be able to sleep.

Ellen pulled on a jump suit over her small, wiry figure. Then she left her room and went outside. Her car was parked not far away. She walked to it, got in, and started the motor. Then she drove away.

As she left Space School and drove out into the country around it, she passed houses where no lights burned. She thought about the people who lived in the houses. They would never board a spaceship and head for the stars. Ellen felt sorry for them. But then a thought crossed her mind. Would *she* get to sail between the stars?

She pressed down on the gas. The car picked up speed.

The answer to her question would come in the morning. If she did pass the test, she would be the happiest person on Earth. If she didn't. . . . She wouldn't let herself think about that.

She drove on without thinking about where she was or where she was going. She just wanted to be doing something. She really didn't know where she was going. She just wanted to drive to pass the time.

As she drove, she looked at her watch. Soon it would be time. She turned the car around and started back toward Space School.

She pulled up to Space School and got out of her car. Walking inside, she knocked on a door.

It was opened at once by a young man. His heavy eyebrows lifted under his wavy black hair. He seemed to be surprised to see Ellen standing there.

"I couldn't sleep," she explained. "So I came to visit you."

Steve Estrada smiled at her. "I couldn't sleep

either. I've been up half the night. Come in, Drake."

She followed him into the apartment and closed the door behind her.

"Come on into the kitchen," Steve called back to her. "Are you hungry?"

"Yes, I am, Estrada, but I don't want to put you to any trouble."

"It's no trouble. I was just about to make breakfast for myself. I'll make something for both of us."

When breakfast was ready, they both sat down and began to eat. For several minutes, they didn't speak to each other.

Finally, Steve asked, "Why couldn't you sleep?"

"Do you really have to ask that question? I couldn't stop thinking about the test we face today."

"You mean you couldn't stop worrying about it, right?"

"It's worth worrying about," Ellen said. "I mean, this is going to be a very special day for both of us. It will either be a good day or a bad day. But either way it will be special."

Steve ate some more eggs, and then he said, "I was born on a farm. Sometimes I can't believe that a farm boy like me might finally become an astronaut."

"I know what you mean," Ellen said. "Sometimes I find it all pretty hard to believe myself. After all, I never thought I'd be a student at Space School. A few years ago, if you'd asked me what I wanted out of life I would have said I didn't know."

"What made you decide?" Steve asked as he drank some milk.

"I'm not really sure," Ellen said. "I guess I love to go places. But John Warshall didn't." She stopped speaking.

"And you were in love with him?"

"Yes."

"What happened?" Steve stopped for a minute. Maybe Ellen didn't want to go into it. "Never mind. It's none of my business."

Ellen said, "He didn't want me to become an astronaut."

Steve said, "When I was just a kid, I wanted to be a policeman. Then I decided to become a doctor. After that, I thought maybe I'd be a teacher. But none of those jobs seemed right for me. I felt I could find something special in life to do."

"I think everyone wants something special

out of life," Ellen told him. "Some people never get it. They're either afraid to try for it, or they think they couldn't get it even if they did try. So they give up. They take what life gives them."

"You're right," Steve said. "But we didn't give up, did we?"

"I suppose we should look at it this way," said Ellen. "If we don't pass the test today, well, that's not the end of the world, is it?"

Steve looked across the table at Ellen. "It will be the end of a dream for me. And for you, too."

"Yes, I guess it would be. I guess I was trying to make myself believe that it doesn't matter. But it does. Very much. I want to get what I've worked and studied so hard for all these years. I want to be an astronaut."

"I wonder what the test will be like?" Steve asked himself more than he did Ellen.

"They never tell you. You just go and face what they have set up for you. I'm pretty sure we're in for a surprise or two."

"So am I." Steve looked out the window. The sun was climbing into the sky. He looked at the clock on the wall. Then he looked at

Ellen. He didn't say anything. He didn't have to speak.

Ellen and Steve got up and put their dishes in the sink. Five minutes later, they both left Steve's apartment.

Together, they began to walk to the place where they would begin the most important test they would take since coming to Space School.

CHAPTER 2

TEST STATION

When they reached the place, they both stopped. In front of them was a red door. The door was set in a big round building. The building, almost a mile high, was large enough to hold a small city.

Above the red door was a sign. Steve looked up at it. So did Ellen. The sign said:

SPACE SCHOOL

TEST STATION

Steve reached out and touched the red door. He thought about the test that he would have

8

to face once he went through the door. If he passed it, he would begin a new life. A life in outer space. He would be able to live a life free of Earth and its problems. He would be free of Earth's crowded cities. He would be free of a planet that too many people had made dirty and ugly.

Ellen's eyes were on the red door. But her mind was on a name. *John Warshall.*

She thought of the man she had loved. Did she love him still? She wasn't really sure. The words he had said to her three years ago rang in her ears again. Those words had been said when she told him she wanted to study at Space School:

"I want a wife who will stay here on Earth with me."

That was what John had said to her then. Later there were more words and finally fights between them. The fights always started because she wanted to become an astronaut. John had said she could have him or the stars. But not both.

She had decided. And now she was here and John was gone. For a minute, she thought of turning away from the red door. She thought of going back—back to John and to. . . .

No! She had worked too hard and studied too long to quit now.

She pushed her thoughts of John away as a man with a beard came toward her.

His name was Validoff. He was the scientist who had made up the test she was about to take.

"Ready?" Validoff asked Ellen and Steve.

"Ready," Steve said.

Ellen said, "Yes, I'm ready," and hoped that what she said was true.

"Both of you know the rules," Validoff said. "Once inside the Test Station, you two are on

your own. You'll have to work together and help each other. You know that you will face danger. But if you pass this last test, both of you will become astronauts."

Validoff looked first at Ellen. Then he looked at Steve. "If either of you wants to back out of this, now is the time to say so. It's not too late, you know." He thought Ellen was about to say something. But she didn't say a word.

Two men walked up. They had space suits for Steve and Ellen.

"OK," Validoff said. "I'll wait at Center Station. And now, one last thing."

"What's that?" Steve asked. He and Ellen began stepping into their space suits.

"Good luck to you, Estrada and Drake," Validoff said and shook hands with them. He left them a minute later when a red light flashed on above the sign.

The red door opened. Ellen walked through the open door into the air lock. Steve followed her inside. The red door closed behind them and locked. Then, the inside door of the air lock opened and they went into the Test Station.

They came into a new world. It was a strange world which Validoff had made to look as much like a world in outer space as possible.

The trees and green grass of Earth were gone. Earth's beautiful blue sky was gone. Gone, too, were all the sounds of Earth. No birds sang. No dogs barked.

Here the sky was a dirty yellow, and there was no sun to be seen. Big rocks lay all over the hard ground. There was no sign of life. Nothing moved. No wind was blowing.

Ellen took a step forward. Then another. Then she turned back to Steve. "The air lock that leads to Center Station is over that way," she said.

Steve joined her. Together they walked on, looking from side to side. Both of them were waiting for something to happen—for the test to begin. They knew it would be hard. To be smart enough wasn't everything. An astronaut had to be able to fight against the dangers of outer space. And to win the fight.

Five minutes later, the fight began for Steve and Ellen. Sharp pieces of ice began to fall from the ugly yellow sky. When they hit the ground, they broke.

A large piece of ice cracked against the face plate in Ellen's space suit. Her eyes grew wide. She touched the glass plate with her hands. But the glass wasn't broken.

"Keep your head down," Steve told her. "If your face plate gets broken. . . ."

"I'll lose my air supply," Ellen said. "And that would mean that I'd. . . ." She didn't finish her sentence. She put her head down. She walked through the ice storm.

Steve slipped on the ice and fell down. Ellen helped him get up again. A few minutes later, she slipped and fell in a pool of water left by the ice. She got up right away.

They walked on as the ice fell down all around them. They could no longer see the ground under their feet. Ice covered it. It was hard to walk. It was almost as hard to just stand still on the ice.

Suddenly, they came to a tall wall of rocks. The wall seemed to reach up and touch the sky.

"Maybe we can go around it," Steve said.

"I don't think that's such a good idea, Estrada. In fact, it would probably be a waste of time. You can't even see where the wall ends. We had better try to climb over it."

Steve looked up at the wall of rocks. Then he looked at Ellen. "OK," he said. "Let's go." He began to climb. But because of all the ice on the rocks, he couldn't hold on to them. He slipped and fell to the ground.

"I'm not as heavy as you are," Ellen said. "Let me go first. Then you climb up behind me. We can go slowly. If I get into trouble during the climb, you can give me a push."

Ellen started up the wall of rocks. Steve came right behind her. All at once, she slipped. Steve caught her legs and held on to them. Ellen held on to the rocks with her hands. Then she began to climb again.

When she was almost at the top of the wall, she yelled down to Steve. "Give me a push!"

Steve did, and she let out a cry of joy.

"I made it!" she shouted. "I made it to the top!" She lay down on the rocks and reached down to Steve.

He took hold of her hands, and she began to pull him up toward the top. Suddenly, several pieces of ice hit Steve's hands. He almost let go of Ellen's hands. But she held on to him. She pulled as hard as she had ever pulled in her life.

Suddenly, Steve found himself on top of the rock wall.

"We made it," Ellen said. "We passed *that* test. And look, Estrada! The ice storm is over." She was right. Soon no more ice fell from the sky.

As they began to climb down the other side of the wall of rocks, Steve spoke in a low voice. "Now what, Drake? Validoff won't let us off this easy."

"Just keep your eyes and ears open," Ellen said. "And keep on walking. But be careful."

The next test was not long in coming. But, when it did come, Ellen and Steve didn't know at first that it *was* a test.

They saw what looked like waves of blue smoke coming toward them. But it wasn't smoke. Instead, it was many small, blue plants. The plants had little white flowers on them. The plants moved along the ground like little blue and white balls. They used their sharp leaves as if they were feet.

Ellen said, "I never saw plants like those before. I'll bet Validoff grew them."

She was about to pick up one of the plants. But Steve caught her arm before she could do so.

"Be careful," he told her. "We don't know anything about these plants. They might cause us trouble."

"But they are so beautiful," Ellen said. "Let's pick some of the flowers to give to Validoff when we get to Center Station."

"No," Steve said. "Don't."

Each of the plants broke into two plants.

"That's how they grow, I guess," he said. "One plant breaks into two, then the two break into four, and so on."

As he spoke, the plants began to crowd around him. They also moved very close to Ellen. One of the plants jumped up. It hit the face plate of Ellen's space suit. It almost cut through the glass of her face plate. She slapped it away from her.

Steve said, "These plants are after our oxygen supply, Ellen. That's why that one almost broke your face plate. They aren't like Earth plants. Earth plants don't breathe oxygen. But these plants breathe it, I guess."

"There isn't much oxygen in the air here," Ellen said. She stepped back from the plants. "That's why the plants are trying to get at *our* oxygen supply."

She hit the plant that jumped toward her face plate.

Then she and Steve began to run. As they ran, they kicked plants out of their way.

But there were many more plants now than there had been at first. And all of them kept coming after Steve and Ellen as they ran.

CHAPTER **3**

THE HARDEST TEST

Steve and Ellen ran on.

Then Steve stopped to throw rocks at the plants. But the rocks didn't stop them. They didn't even hurt them. Steve decided that rocks were not the answer to the problem of the plants.

"Run faster! It's our only hope," Ellen yelled to him. But the plants stayed right behind them.

"We have one thing going for us," Ellen gasped. She felt as if her heart were about to give out on her. "We are getting close to Center Station."

"Oh, no!" Steve shouted. He slowed down and then stopped running.

"Steve!" Ellen shouted at him. *"Don't give up!"*

"Look, Drake!" Steve said.

Then Ellen saw why he had come to a stop. In front of them were *more* plants. Hundreds of plants were in front of them. And there were also hundreds behind them. And they were cut off from Center Station.

Ellen said, "Maybe we could let a little oxygen out of our space suits. That might keep the plants from coming after us." She hit at the plants to keep them off her space suit.

"There wouldn't be enough oxygen for all of them," Steve said. "If there were only some way to get more oxygen into the air here, we would be safe. The plants would leave us alone then." He knocked a plant off his chest.

"Maybe we could burn the plants up," Ellen said. "No, that wouldn't work. The fire would use up every bit of oxygen that's left in the air. It would need the oxygen to burn. I don't know what. . . ."

"I've got an idea!" Steve yelled. He kicked at the plants near him. "Water has oxygen in it!"

Ellen shook her head. "There isn't any water around here. There are no lakes. No rivers."

"Drake, we have to go back the way we came."

"No! Center Station is in *front* of us. If we go back, those plants will kill us."

"We *have* to go back," Steve said a second time.

"No, Estrada!" Ellen shouted again.

"Please! Do as I say!" Steve said. "Come back with me."

But Ellen wouldn't. Instead, she ran forward through the plants. They made her fall down. She screamed.

Steve ran to her. He pulled the plants from her body and forced her to her feet. Then he caught her arm and pulled her along with him.

"Estrada, don't!" she shouted. "We can't go back. We *must* not!"

Steve didn't say anything. He just kept pulling her along, kicking at the plants in his way.

It took them some time to get to the place Steve was headed for. When Ellen saw where they were, she let out a cry. Once again they stood before the wall of rocks.

"Climb!" Steve shouted. "Climb for your life!"

Ellen climbed up the wall. He climbed right behind her. Sometimes he fell a short way. Sometimes Ellen did. But finally they made it to the top of the wall. They half climbed and half fell down the other side.

"I don't understand!" Ellen said. "Why come all the way back here?"

Steve pointed to the top of the rock wall. "Look." There was a smile on his face. The plants were on top of the wall. They began to climb down toward Steve and Ellen.

Steve didn't move. Ellen started to back away. She fell on some pieces of ice that had come down during the ice storm. Steve didn't help her get up. He just watched her. She picked up a piece of ice. She looked at it, then at Steve, then at the ice again. The ice began to turn to water in her hand. She looked up at Steve and began to laugh.

"This ice. . . . Most of it has turned to water," she said.

"And much of the water has been taken up into the air."

Ellen laughed again. "Water is full of oxygen. So now the air here has a lot of oxygen in it. I didn't even think about the ice storm."

"Look at the plants," Steve said. "They are

getting oxygen from the water and from the air."

"Which means that now we can get out of here and go on to Center Station," Ellen said.

"We have another climb first," Steve said. "So let's get to it."

He and Ellen climbed the wall of rocks for a third time. At the top, Ellen took one last look at the plants that had almost killed them. Then she and Steve climbed down the other side of the wall. They headed for Center Station.

"I wonder what's in store for us next," Ellen said. Her voice was little more than a whisper.

"Maybe nothing more," Steve said. "Maybe now we're home free."

As they walked on, they came to a lake.

"That lake is the first nice thing I've seen here in the Test Station," Ellen said. "It's lovely, isn't it?"

Steve was about to speak when the water in the lake moved. He watched it. So did Ellen. But both of them kept on walking as they watched. Suddenly, a great fish put its head out of the water.

"That's the biggest fish I've ever seen!" Steve said.

"It looks more like a bird than a fish," Ellen said.

The fish moved through the water toward them. Steve and Ellen backed away from the lake.

Steve said, "We'd better get out of here. I don't like the looks of that fish—or bird-fish."

Ellen took Steve's hand, and they were both about to run when the fish opened its mouth. Fire came out of the fish's mouth. It caused Ellen to duck down and to let go of Steve's hand.

The fish lifted its head high above the water. It sent more fire flying toward Steve and Ellen. Steve ran one way. Ellen ran another.

The fish went after Steve. Fire flew from its mouth. Once the fire almost touched Steve, but he got away from it just in time. He ran away from the lake, hoping that the fish couldn't leave the lake. If it could, he didn't have a chance.

He ran some more and then looked back. The fish was gone from sight—the water in the lake didn't move.

He came to a stop and looked around. He was glad the fish was gone. But where was Ellen? He couldn't see her. He called her name

as loud as he could. But he got no answer.

He began to look for her. As he looked, he kept calling her name. But she didn't answer. He began to be afraid. Not for himself, but for Ellen. Maybe, he thought, the fish had hurt her with its fire.

He would have to go back near the lake to see if she was there. He really didn't want to go near the lake. But he began to walk back toward it. When he came close to it, the fish lifted its head above the water again. Before it could shoot fire at him, Steve ran.

But he had found out what he wanted to know. Ellen wasn't near the lake. He didn't know where she was. He called her name again. But it wasn't Ellen who answered him. It was a short, fat man. The man wore glasses.

"Hello, there," he said to Steve. "Nice day, isn't it?"

Steve was as surprised as a person could be. He never thought he would see another person here in the Test Station. Validoff had not said that there were other students being tested here today. And he wasn't wearing a space suit!

"I'd stay away from that lake if I were you," the man said with a smile. "There's a fish in it that can. . . ."

"Shoot fire at people," Steve said, finishing what the man had been about to say. "Who are you? Why don't you have a space suit on?"

The man waved a hand as if to make Steve's questions go away. "You're Steve Estrada," he said.

"Yes, I am. How do you know me? I never saw you before in my life."

"Maybe you just don't remember meeting

me," the man said. "But that doesn't matter. What *does* matter is what I can do for you."

"I hope that you can help me find my friend," Steve said. "Her name is Ellen Drake, and she's gone. I mean I've lost her. When the fish came after us. . . ."

"I'm not interested in anyone but you," the man said. "I've come to do something for you."

Steve waited for the man to go on, but his mind was on Ellen.

"Come over here with me," the man said as he led Steve to a big rock. "Take a look in that box of mine."

Steve picked up the box that sat on the rock. He looked inside it. He couldn't believe his eyes!

In the box was more money than he had ever seen in his life.

"It's all yours, Estrada," the man said.

"Mine?"

"Yes. It's yours, that is, if you'll do something to earn it."

"Like what?" Steve asked.

"Leave Space School. Give up your idea of becoming an astronaut. Never leave Earth."

"I couldn't do that! I'd *never* do that!"

The man took the box from Steve. "Then

I'm afraid you can't have this money. By the way, do you know how much money is in this box?"

Steve shook his head.

"One million dollars," the man said.

"Why do you want to give it to me? Why do you want me to leave Space School?"

"I won't answer those questions," the man said. "Think about what this money could mean to you. You would never have to work a day in your life. You could buy anything you want—*everything* you want. Think about that, Steve Estrada."

Steve did think about it. He thought about fast cars and fine food and a beautiful place to live. He thought about being free to do what he wanted to do, to go where he wanted to go.

"Will you leave Space School?" the man asked him.

Steve looked down at the box in the man's hands. And at the million dollars that were inside it.

CHAPTER 4

I LOVE YOU

Ellen finally stopped running. She was able at last to catch her breath. She pushed thoughts of the fish from her mind. She thought about Steve instead.

She had thought he was right behind her as she ran from the lake. But when she looked back, he was not in sight. She would have to go back and try to find him.

She started to return to the lake, looking carefully around, not sure what might happen to her next. And Steve was not here so they could help each other if they got in trouble.

That thought brought another one to her

mind. Could she pass any more tests alone? She began to walk as fast as she could. She called Steve's name.

When she was in sight of the lake, she stopped and looked all around. Steve wasn't there. She was about to turn away from the lake when something caught her eye.

It was a tall man. He was far away, but Ellen was sure that she knew who he was. She began to walk toward him—and then began to run toward him. He saw her coming and ran to meet her. They threw their arms around one another.

"John Warshall!" Ellen said. "How did you get *here?* What are you doing here? I never thought I'd see you again."

"I couldn't let you go," John said. "I love you too much, Ellen. So I came looking for you. I don't want you to go on with all this. I want you to leave here and come away with me. We were very happy together before you came to Space School. Leave it now and we can be happy together again."

Ellen let go of John and looked up at him. "We're right back where we were before, aren't we? You won't really love me until I give up my plan to become an astronaut, will you?"

"I've told you a hundred times how I feel," John said. "Let's leave here and go."

He went on talking. As he did, his words made Ellen wish that there was some way she could have him and her new life at the same time.

She remembered how happy they had once been together. Her love for him made her heart feel as if it were about to break.

But she knew what she was going to do and say. She ran her small hands through his red hair. She pulled him down toward her and whispered in his ear.

"I love you, John, but I have to leave you. I'm sorry. You'll never know how sorry I am about this. But this is the way it has to be. Good-bye, John."

She turned away from him. Tears came to her eyes as she walked away. She stopped, turned, and looked back. But he was gone.

She took a deep breath and walked on. She called Steve's name several times. She began to think she would never see him again. But just then she heard her name called. She knew who was calling her. She knew that voice very well. It was Steve's!

"Estrada!" she yelled as loud as she could. "I'm here. Where are you?"

Suddenly, there he was, coming through the rocks toward her. She ran to meet him.

"I've been looking all over for you," he told her when she reached him. "Are you OK?"

"Yes. What about you?"

"I'm fine. But you're not going to believe this. I just met a man who said he would give me a million dollars if I would leave Space School. When I told him I wouldn't take his money, he went away."

"A strange thing happened to me, too," Ellen said. She told Steve about her meeting with John Warshall.

"You say he wanted you to go away with him?"

Yes, he did. But I wouldn't."

"I don't understand all this," Steve said. "How did your friend get into the Test Station? How did that man with the million dollars get in here?"

"Let's head for Center Station," Ellen said. "Maybe Validoff knows the answers."

Half an hour later, they reached Center Station. At its air lock, they stopped. Ellen put her fingers against the door of the lock, and so did Steve.

The door read the prints of their fingers. It opened. They went through the lock and into Center Station where they took off their space suits. Ellen sat down in a chair. Steve also sat down and closed his eyes.

He opened them when he heard Validoff say, "Welcome to Center Station. You made it. You both passed your tests."

Ellen and Steve both stood up. Validoff shook hands with them.

Then he said, "You had a hard time out there, Drake and Estrada. But you had to go through it all. You may find things in outer space that are even worse than those you just faced."

"That ice storm was really something," Ellen said.

"Such storms happen on some of the planets in outer space," Validoff said. "Now you know what they're like and how to live through them."

"I didn't like that ice storm at all," Steve said. "But I liked those nasty plants even less."

Validoff said, "As you know, those plants breathe oxygen. If oxygen is in short supply, they'll do anything to get some. That means trouble for humans. I grew those plants myself. We ship them to other planets where the people use them for food."

"I hope we've seen the last of them," Ellen said. "And to think that I wanted to pick the flowers for you! I'm glad Steve didn't let me."

Validoff smiled.

"The ice storm, the plants, and the bird-fish were bad enough," Steve said. "But the man was a real problem for me. I almost took the money he was going to give me. I almost gave up my plans to become an astronaut."

"I met my friend, John Warshall, out there," Ellen began and then she looked at Validoff. "How did he get into the Test Station?"

"And the man with the money," Steve said. "How did *he* get in?"

"That wasn't John Warshall out there," Validoff said to Ellen. "It was a robot made to look and talk like him. It was to test you. We wanted to know if you could be talked out of becoming an astronaut."

"A robot!" Steve said. "Then the man with the money was also a robot, right?"

"You're right," Validoff said. "That was *your* last test, Steve."

"But how did you know about John?" Ellen asked Validoff.

He said, "We check on the lives of all our students. We learned about him and made the robot to test you."

"That robot certainly did look just like John!" Ellen said.

Validoff smiled again. "Now that you've both passed your tests, it's time to talk about other things."

Steve asked, "Just what did you have in mind?"

"I think you know. So I'll get right to the point. As you both know, we want you to build an Earth Colony on Planet 1 of Star 84 in Galaxy 5. Your spaceship is ready for you. And, as you also know, the first ship we sent out has been lost. We can't find it. We don't know what's happened to it. I hope you two will have better luck than the astronauts on that first ship."

"When do we leave?" Ellen asked.

"Tomorrow," Validoff told her. "First, you'll need some rest after all you've been through today."

CHAPTER **5**

OUT TO THE STARS

It was a long night for Steve. He lay awake
through most of it. His mind was full of
thoughts of what the next day would bring.
When the next day came, he would be free. He
would be free to climb up to the stars.

At last he fell asleep. He dreamed. His dream
was both strange and wonderful. He dreamed
that he sat on a large, white horse. After he
spoke soft words in the horse's ear, it jumped
the fence in front of it. The horse took Steve,
not across fields, but up—up into the sky. Steve

rode the horse past the stars. All around them was rich music, the sweet songs that the stars sang.

But then Steve woke up. The horse was gone. So were the stars. His dream was dead.

No, he thought, my dream is *not* dead. I am about to begin a new dream, an even better one. Instead of a horse, I will ride a spaceship to all the worlds there are.

He got up and dressed as fast as he could. He ate his breakfast and then went to Center Station. Ellen was already there. So was Validoff.

"Good morning," Steve said to them. "Is the ship ready?"

"It is," said Validoff. "And I can see that you're ready, too."

"It seems to me," Steve said, "that I've been ready for this minute all my life."

"Can we go on board now?" Ellen asked Validoff. Her eyes were bright, and she couldn't seem to stand still.

Validoff led the way out of the room. Outside, the ship stood waiting.

As Steve walked toward it, he thought of a toy. The ship might have been a great toy—one made for the children of giants to play with. But this ship was *his* toy. His and Drake's. He felt his heart begin to beat fast. He could almost hear it beat inside his chest.

The ship didn't look like the ones scientists had made when Steve and Ellen had started Space School. Those spaceships weren't as big as this one. This spaceship had more jets than the old ones had. It also had large, dark windows that could be seen through when they were lighted. The ship didn't point up at the sky. It sat on the ground like a round airplane, but it had no wheels. Instead of wheels, it would use its jets for lift-offs and landings.

There was what looked like a small ship on top of it. But the part that looked like a second ship was really part of the ship itself. Steve and Ellen would eat and sleep there. They would work in the bottom part of the ship.

The ship's name was painted on its side: VOYAGER.

Ellen had been walking beside Steve. Now she was far in front of him. She almost ran toward the ship. She climbed the steps that led to the ship. Soon she was out of sight.

Steve and Validoff climbed up the steps. They went inside the ship. Steve had been on board the ship many times while he was a student at Space School. But every time he came on board, he felt as if he had come into a new world.

There were two large, fixed chairs facing two giant windows in the big control room. The windows were black until they were switched on for viewing the outside. There were also two large video screens and one smaller zoom video screen for space close-ups. Now they were gray. But when the ship left Earth, the screens would give views of space objects.

On the right side of the room was the ship's control board. It had many lights of different colors on it. It also had dials and buttons. The control board was the very heart of the ship.

"Run a check on Voyager's systems," Validoff said. "Make sure that everything is in order."

Steve and Ellen began to check out the ship.

Steve tested the control board. All the lights went on. He tested the dials. They all worked. Then Ellen tested the gravity control system. It was fine. So was the emergency gravity control system.

Ellen checked the giant windows and video screens. When she turned them on, they showed Center Station just outside. Then Steve checked Voyager's signal system. It was in good shape. They could use the signal system to talk to Earth from outer space. They could also use it to talk to other planets where there was life. And to other ships in outer space.

Steve went into the next room. He checked

the 100 big glass boxes that filled it.

In each of the glass boxes was a person. The people in the boxes didn't move. Their eyes were closed. The scientists had put all of them into a deep sleep. They wouldn't wake up until Voyager completed its trip. When they did wake up, they would build an Earth Colony on Planet 1 of Star 84 in Galaxy 5.

Steve returned to the control room. Then he and Ellen checked the air in the ship. They also checked the food that had been brought on board Voyager.

Then they went up to the top of the ship. They looked at their rooms. All was in order. Then they returned to the control room. Validoff was waiting for them.

"Everything is fine," Ellen told him.

"We should check in with Voyager," Steve said. He spoke to the ship. "Voyager, can you hear me?"

"I CAN HEAR YOU," Voyager said. "WHAT DO YOU WANT, ESTRADA?"

The ship's clear voice rang out all around them. It wasn't a woman's voice. It wasn't a man's voice. It was something of both. The ship's voice was like the voice of a bell that could ring in words instead of just sounds.

The sound of Voyager speaking surprised Steve. He knew that the ship was not just a machine. He knew that it had been given more than a voice by the scientists. In a way, Voyager was almost human. Steve thought of Voyager as a person. A person with a mind but with the body of a ship. There had never before been a ship like Voyager. None of the other ships in the past could talk or think for themselves. Still, when Voyager spoke, Steve found himself surprised.

"We've checked everything on board," he said to Voyager.

"Everything is in order," Ellen said. "We just want to know if you find things in order too."

"I DO," said Voyager.

"Then we are ready for lift-off," Ellen said.

"YES, WE ARE," Voyager said. "LIFT-OFF WILL TAKE PLACE IN 30 MINUTES."

Validoff said, "That means that I must leave you now." He crossed the control room. At the door that led outside, he stopped. He turned back to Steve and Ellen and said, "Good luck, Estrada. Good luck, Drake."

"Thank you," Ellen said.

"Good-bye," Steve said.

Validoff gave them each a gentle slap on the back. Then he was gone.

Steve went over to the control board. Ellen sat down in front of the small video screen. Both of them checked their systems again.

Time passed.

"TWO MINUTES UNTIL LIFT-OFF," Voyager said. "GET READY, PLEASE."

Lights flashed on the control board in front of Steve. He pushed a button. A green light went on at the top of the board.

Ellen turned on the giant window lights and the video screens.

"LIFT-OFF!" said Voyager and Steve at the same time.

The ship's many jets fired. Outside, the noise was very loud. But inside the ship, Steve and Ellen couldn't hear it.

Voyager began to climb into the sky. On the video screen, Ellen could see the wide blue sky and the sun.

"We are miles from Earth already," Steve said. He kept his eyes on the control board. "Soon we will be in outer space."

The video screen no longer showed blue sky. Now there was no sun on the screen. Ellen looked again through the large windows in the control room. Below Voyager, Earth was getting smaller and smaller. It looked like a basketball. Near Earth was an even smaller ball. It was the moon.

In a low voice, Ellen whispered, "Good-bye."

But Steve heard what she had said. He joined her at the windows.

"WE ARE NOW 210 MILES FROM EARTH," Voyager said.

"Is something wrong, Drake?" Steve asked. He put his hand on her shoulder.

She shook her head. "No." It was a lie and

she knew it. She looked at Steve. "We're leaving our old life behind."

Steve waited for her to go on.

She said, "I may never see John again."

"Do you really want to?"

"I don't know."

"Are you sorry now? About leaving him?'

"To be free isn't always easy," Ellen said. "People need other people."

"Not me," Steve said with a shake of his head. "I don't need anyone."

Ellen was about to say something to him. But Voyager's voice sounded.

The ship said, "I HAVE MADE LUNCH FOR YOU. PLEASE COME AND EAT NOW."

Ellen and Steve left the control room. They climbed the steps to the top of the ship.

"What did you make for lunch, Voyager?" Ellen asked.

Voyager answered, "MEAT, VEGETABLES, AND PIE. THE MEAT IS NOT EARTH MEAT. BUT YOU MUST LEARN TO EAT STRANGE FOODS NOW. THE VEGETABLES ARE FROM EARTH. AND THE PIE IS MADE WITH APPLES, ALSO FROM EARTH. NOW YOU WILL PLEASE SIT DOWN AND EAT YOUR LUNCH."

They ate. When they had finished, Ellen

said, "Voyager, that was very good. You're the best cook on Earth."

"THAT IS INCORRECT," Voyager said. "I AM THE BEST COOK IN SPACE." Ellen laughed. Then to Steve, she said, "I think I'll go to my room."

"OK," Steve said. "I'll see you later." He returned to the control room.

Voyager broke into his thoughts. "THERE IS A STORM COMING. I WILL HAVE TO CHANGE COURSE."

"A storm?"

In her room, Ellen had heard what Voyager said. Her voice came through the ship's signal system. "What kind of storm is it, Voyager?"

"A METEOR STORM. I HAVE NOW CHANGED COURSE. THE STORM SHOULD MISS US."

But Voyager had not changed course in time. The meteors still flew towards the ship.

Ellen came into the control room. She and Steve looked at the video screen. On the screen, there were hundreds of meteors coming towards them. Each one was like a big stone.

"I MUST CHANGE COURSE AGAIN," Voyager said.

But before the course could be changed, meteors began to strike Voyager.

CHAPTER **6**

TROUBLE ON THE SHIP

Red lights flashed on Voyager's control board. Steve made a note of each light. Each light told him where a meteor had hit Voyager.

"Drake," he said, "one of the air locks has opened. It's the one on the left side of the ship."

Ellen didn't waste any time. She left the room and was gone for some time. When she returned, she said, "I've closed the lock. We can fix it later." She looked up at the screen.

The screen showed a very large meteor. It was flying toward Voyager.

Suddenly, the lights went out as the meteor hit the ship. Then they came back on. A red light went on in front of Steve. "The meteor that just hit us broke our gravity control system," he said.

He pushed a button on the control board. Then pushed the button again.

"The gravity control system is still broken," he said. "I'll have to go to emergency gravity control." He was about to turn a dial. But before he could, he began to float up into the air. So did Ellen. She turned over and over. With their gravity control system broken, they couldn't stand on the ground. They had no weight.

Steve bumped into a wall. He kicked the wall. The kick sent him floating across the room. He came to the control board. As he floated by it, he grabbed the top of it. He held on. Then he reached down to the dial he was after.

"Drake!" he yelled. "Get as close to the floor as you can. I'm going to turn on our emergency gravity control system."

Ellen kicked at the wall. She floated down towards the floor. Steve turned the dial.

Gravity returned to the ship. Ellen dropped to the floor. She didn't fall far because she was almost touching the floor when gravity returned.

Steve dropped to the floor. He landed on his feet.

"THE STORM IS OVER," Voyager said. "I WILL NOW GET BACK ON COURSE. PLEASE CHECK MY SYSTEMS. FIX ANYTHING THAT IS BROKEN."

Steve and Ellen went to work to fix the broken air lock. It took them almost an hour. But when they were finished, it worked perfectly. Then they spent time on the broken gravity control system. When it was fixed, Steve turned it on.

Voyager said, "I SEE A SHIP TO OUR LEFT. I HAVE NOT RECEIVED A SIGNAL FROM IT. IT DOES NOT ANSWER WHEN I SIGNAL IT."

Steve looked at the video screen. On it was a spaceship.

When she saw it, Ellen let out a cry. "I know that ship! That's the first ship that was sent out. It's the one Validoff said was lost."

"It's not lost now," Steve said. "We've found it. Voyager, let's dock with that ship."

Voyager began to fly to the left. Soon Voyager was flying close to the other ship.

Steve and Ellen went to the air lock they had fixed. They waited for Voyager to dock with the other ship.

But then Voyager said, "I CANNOT DOCK. MY DOCKING MACHINE IS OUT OF ORDER."

Steve ran to the control board to check the docking machine. But he couldn't control it. He went back and told Ellen, "I'll have to go outside to fix our docking machine."

He put on his space suit.

"Estrada," Ellen said, "I'll stay at the control board for as long as you'll be outside. While you're gone, I'll take care of things here."

He went into the air lock and closed the door behind him. He connected a lifeline to his space suit. The other end of his lifeline was connected to the air lock's wall.

He opened the outer door of the lock and floated out into space. Because there was no gravity in space, he could only float.

All around him it was black. Here and there a star made a bright point of light in the blackness. There was not a sound to be heard. Without air to carry sound waves, space was without any noise at all.

The silence pounded in Steve's ears. He wanted to shout, to make some kind of sound to end the silence. But he didn't. He knew he couldn't make any sound here where there was no air at all.

He caught hold of one of the handles on the side of the ship. They had been put there for times like this. He caught one handle after another in order to move along the side of Voyager. Finally, he reached the docking machine.

He opened a little door in Voyager's side. He took out some tools and began to fix the docking machine. At last, he had finished. He started to put his tools back into the side of Voyager.

Then he dropped one. He watched it float out into space.

In anger, Steve kicked the side of Voyager. He let go of the handle and floated out to grab the lost tool. His lifeline kept him connected to the ship. But the tool floated out of his reach.

He let himself float on. He had almost reached the tool when something caught his eye. As he rolled over, he saw a meteor flying toward him. He rolled over again to get out of its way. He pulled on his lifeline. The meteor missed him.

But it cut his lifeline in two.

He floated away from Voyager. He couldn't help himself.

Inside Voyager, Ellen was watching the video screen. When she saw what had just happened to Steve, she wasted no time. She put on her space suit, ran to the air lock, and connected a lifeline to her suit. Then she floated out into space.

Steve was far from Voyager now. Ellen floated out after him. Her hands reached out for him. But she couldn't reach him. She felt her lifeline grow stiff. She had come as far as she could. But she still couldn't reach Steve.

At first, she felt fear as she watched Steve

float away from her. Then she felt angry. She would have to do something, she decided. She *couldn't* let Steve die out here in space. But what could she do?

The thought came to her in a flash. She wished she had thought of it before. She could speak to Voyager on her space suit radio. She reached for the small radio and gave orders to Voyager.

Voyager did what Ellen had ordered. The ship moved closer to Steve.

Now, Ellen was able to reach Steve. She caught him with one hand. With the other hand, she pulled on her lifeline. She got both herself and Steve back into the lock.

They went inside Voyager and took off their space suits. They just stood there looking at one another for a minute. Then Ellen said, "A funny thing happened to me out there, Estrada. For a minute, I thought you were John Warshall."

Then Steve spoke. When he did, his voice was low. His eyes were on Ellen. "I was wrong about what I said before, Drake. I mean about my not needing anyone. I sure did need you a little while ago. Thanks for helping me. Thanks a lot."

He pulled her small frame close to his chest. Ellen couldn't help herself. She put her arms around him and held on for several minutes. Then she let him go.

She smiled at him. "You're welcome," she said.

"I fixed the docking machine," Steve told her. "Now we can dock with the lost ship."

"I STILL HAVE NOT BEEN ABLE TO REACH ANYONE ON THAT SHIP," Voyager said. "SOMETHING MUST BE WRONG THERE."

"Let's dock with the ship," Steve said. "Ellen and I will go on board and see what's wrong."

Voyager began to dock with the lost ship.

CHAPTER 7

"WE NEED HELP!"

Both ships flew on after they had docked.

"Should we get in our space suits to go on board?" Ellen asked Steve.

"I don't think we need to."

"But what if. . . ." Ellen said no more. She decided Steve was right. They probably wouldn't need their suits on board the lost ship. It would have oxygen. They went through the air lock and into the lost ship.

At once they went to the ship's control room. They found the two women who had been in control of the ship. Both of them were dead.

One lay against the control board, and the other lay on the floor beside it.

"What happened to them?" Ellen wondered.

Steve shook his head. "I don't know. But I think there's something wrong with the air in here. I don't think there's enough oxygen in it."

"Then we'd better get into our space suits," Ellen said.

"You're right," Steve said. "I can't breathe very well."

They returned to Voyager and suited up. Then they went back on board the lost ship. They went from place to place on the ship. They came into a room. Broken glass lay all over the floor. Once the glass had been a wall.

Steve read the words on the plate above the broken glass. "Plants were kept in here," he said when he finished reading. "They were supposed to get a lot of oxygen." He then looked at the dial below the plate. "This dial shows that only a little oxygen was sent into the room."

"I don't understand all this," Ellen said. "What kind of plants were kept here? Who broke the glass? Where are the plants now?"

As if in answer to her questions, several small blue plants moved slowly into the room.

There were white flowers all over them.

"Estrada!" Ellen shouted. "*Look!*"

He turned from the dial and saw the plants. "Now I get it," he said. "Those plants are the same as the ones that were in the Test Station." He looked at the broken glass on the floor. "They didn't get enough oxygen in the room where they were kept. So they...."

"So they cut through the glass," Ellen said. "They wanted to get out of the room so they could breathe the oxygen in the ship."

"That would be my guess," Steve said. "This ship must have been taking the plants to another planet."

"Validoff did say that some people on other planets ate these plants," Ellen said.

"I don't think we have to worry about *these* plants," Steve said. "Look at them. They're almost dead."

"I'm glad of that," Ellen said. "Very glad."

"I wonder if the other people on board are OK," Steve said.

Ellen went with him to the room that was like the room on Voyager. It too was filled with glass boxes. But these boxes were all broken. The people inside the boxes were dead.

"The plants did this," Ellen said. "They

wanted the oxygen inside those boxes. So they cut through the glass to get it."

Steve didn't say anything. He walked slowly back to the air lock. There was nothing he could do for the people on the ship. It was too late for them.

Ellen walked over to him. She guessed what he was thinking. "It's the same on Earth as it is here. Everything fights to live. Animals kill each other for food. People kill animals. Sometimes people kill each other."

"I know," Steve said in a soft voice. "I guess I hoped outer space would be different. But I knew it wouldn't be."

"It *is* different," Ellen said. "But it's also the same as Earth in some ways."

They had reached the air lock. Steve was about to step into it when he saw plants inside it. "Ellen, help me get those plants out of there."

Together they threw all the plants out of the lock into the lost ship.

"OK," Steve said. "Open our lock now."

Ellen did. Steve started to close the other lock. But before he could close it all the way, some plants got inside. They moved past Ellen and into Voyager.

Steve shut the lock. He ran with Ellen into Voyager.

The plants were stronger now because of the oxygen in Voyager's air. They began to grow. Each one broke into two plants. Ellen threw them into the air lock. She shut the door on them.

"That won't help now," Steve yelled.

"But we have to do *something!*" Ellen yelled back. "These plants will use up all of our oxygen. We'll die if they do."

Suddenly a plant jumped into the air. It smashed against Steve's face plate. He slapped it away.

Ellen was fighting with some of the plants. They were all around her.

"Our oxygen won't last much longer," Steve said. "We need help."

"But there isn't anyone here to help us. Estrada, what can we do?"

He didn't answer Ellen. There was no answer he could give her. They had won their fight against the plants in the Test Station on Earth. But they were about to lose their fight this time, he thought.

He hit the plants that were trying to cut the glass of his face plate. The plants' sharp leaves sounded like tiny stones pounding against the glass. As he hit the plants away, others took their places.

Suddenly, some of the plants stopped moving. Then others also stopped. Steve couldn't believe what he saw. *Some of the plants were dead!*

"I don't understand this," he said. He shook his head from side to side. "What's killing them?"

Soon all the plants were dead.

"YOU MAY THANK ME." It was the clear voice of Voyager.

"Thank you, Voyager," Steve said. "But I still don't understand. What did you do?"

"I TOOK ALL THE OXYGEN OUT OF THE AIR. I DO NOT BREATHE OXYGEN, AS YOU KNOW. YOU TWO HAD YOUR OWN SUPPLY OF OXYGEN IN YOUR SUITS. I THOUGHT ABOUT THE PROBLEM. IT WAS A SIMPLE PROBLEM, REALLY."

"Not for me, it wasn't," Steve said. "Without your help, we would have been killed."

"I WILL NOW PUT THE OXYGEN BACK INTO THE AIR," Voyager said. "YOU TWO MAY TAKE OFF YOUR SPACE SUITS." And they did.

Steve said, "I'm sure glad that's over." As he looked at Ellen, he thought, I'm glad to be on this ship with you instead of just by myself.

"Estrada, let's take a rest break."

Voyager said, "I AM VERY SORRY, DRAKE AND ESTRADA, BUT THIS IS NO TIME TO REST. YOU MUST GET THESE DEAD PLANTS OUT OF HERE. YOU MUST CHECK ALL MY SYSTEMS. WE MUST GET TO PLANET 1 OF STAR 84 IN GALAXY 5. LATER YOU CAN REST."

Ellen looked at Steve. He gave her a smile. Then they both began to put the dead plants on board the lost ship. Soon all the plants were gone.

To Ellen's great surprise, so were her thoughts of John Warshall. He belonged to Earth. She belonged to the stars.

As if to prove that she was right, Voyager left the lost ship and flew on toward Galaxy 5.